CARL GOES TO DAYCARE

CARL GOES TO DAYCARE

ALEXANDRA DAY

FARRAR STRAUS GIROUX
NEW YORK

Also by Alexandra Day

Carl Goes Shopping
Carl's Christmas
Carl's Afternoon in the Park
Carl's Masquerade

To All Saints', San Diego, both church and school, for all the good services they have rendered to me and my family over the years

In particular, for enthusiastically enacting the scenes in this book, I am very grateful to Willi, the two Maureens, Katherine So and her assistants, and All Saints' Preschool students Sarah Steadman, Kristen Carter, Josie and Angelina Giacalone, Vincenzo Ruffino, Christopher Feuling Ferguson, Sean Ziebarth, David Lockwood, Mariano Bradford, Lucas Matkowski, Emily Lemasters, Nicole Heckathorne, and Benjamin Cooper

And affectionate thanks to my friend Cooper Edens, that brilliant idea man who started this book on its path.

Library of Congress catalog card number: 93-17256
Published in Canada by HarperCollins*CanadaLtd*
Color separations by Photolitho AG
Printed and bound in the United States by Berryville Graphics
First edition, 1993

The Carl character originally appeared in *Good Dog, Carl*
by Alexandra Day, published by Green Tiger Press

"We're happy to have Carl and Madeleine visit us this morning. We're about to start on music time. I'm sure they won't be any trouble at all."

"You be good, Carl, and help Mrs. Manning with the children. I'll be back in a little while."

SHAPING UP

TODAY'S ACTIVITIES
FREE PLAY
MUSIC CIRCLE
TRAFFIC SAFETY GAME
PRACTICE "Teddy Bears' Picnic" for Parent
WORK ON OUR
SNACK

STOP

OUR PETS
YIELD
OP
ONE
WAY

OUR PETS

PRACTICE "Teddy Bears' Picnic" for Parents' Day

WORK ON OUR GARD

SNACK

CLEANUP

NAP

STORY HOUR

OUTDOOR PLAY

OUR GARDEN
DAISIES
POPPIES
LEAVES
BUGS

OUR GARDEN

OUR GARDEN
TULIPS
DAFFODILS
DAISIES

PRACTICE "Teddy Bears' Picnic" for Parents' Day
WORK ON OUR GARDEN
SNACK
CLEANUP
NAP

STOP
STEMS
LEAVES
BUGS
BUTTER-
FLIES

CARL,
OPEN
THE DOOR

"Carl! What on earth have you been up to?"

"Oh, Carl's been wonderful.
I'm so glad he was here!"